The Red
Comb

Sponsorship for the production of the Spanish edition was provided by the Committee on
Literature for Women and Children of Intermedia/National Council of Churches U.S.A.

Translation and adaptation by Argentina Palacios.

Published by Troll Medallion, an imprint and trademark of Troll Communications L.L.C.

First published in the English language in the United States by BridgeWater Books.

Printed in the United States of America.

10 9 8 7 6 5 4 3 2 1

Library of Congress Cataloging-in-Publication Data
Picó, Fernando.
The red comb / by Fernando Picó; illustrated by María Antonia Ordóñez;
[translation by Argentina Palacios].
p.   cm.
Summary: In mid-nineteenth-century Puerto Rico, an old woman and a young village girl
conspire to save a runaway African slave by passing her off as the woman's niece.
ISBN 0-8167-3539-5 (lib. bdg.)   ISBN 0-8167-3540-9 (pbk.)
[1. Fugitive slaves—Fiction.   2. Blacks—Puerto Rico—Fiction.   3. Puerto Rico—Fiction.]
I. Ordóñez, María Antonia, ill.   II. Title
PZ7.P5529Re   1994   [Fic]—dc20   94-9832

The Red Comb

by Fernando Picó

Illustrated by María Antonia Ordóñez

Troll Medallion

Pedro Calderón was the envy of all the young men who lived near Río Piedras, Puerto Rico. He received eight *pesos* for each runaway slave he captured and turned over to the local authorities. With such a handsome reward, a man could buy a cow or an acre of land, or pay a month's wages to one of his farmhands. And Calderón had been lucky enough to catch four runaways in less than two years. The villagers envied his good fortune.

"He could at least leave one for the rest of us," grumbled Nepomuceno, the muleteer. "If I could catch just one slave and claim the reward, I would celebrate my daughter's wedding in grand style."

"Have you forgotten that our grandparents came to this island on a tiny, waterlogged boat after fleeing from an Englishman's plantation in Antigua?" scolded old Rosa Bultrón. "What would have become of them if Pedro Calderón had been alive in those days?"

"But that was different, *siña* Rosa," said Nepomuceno. "Our elders were good people who ran away from other islands. The runaways who show up in our village are lawbreakers. They steal our eggs and our crops. And the soldiers come after them and disturb our fields trying to track them down."

Rosa Bultrón shook her head. "Hunting down black slaves and turning them over to the mayor is no business for black folks. Even if they steal our food, they're only trying to survive. Black folks should help black folks, not hurt them."

But Nepomuceno and the others were not so sure. Pedro Calderón was a wealthy man. He invited everyone in the town to a dance now and then. He was always ready with a joke or a story. Sometimes he even lent his ox at plowing time.

The runaways who appeared asking for food and a place to sleep were strangers. Sometimes the words that came out of their mouths were hard to understand. And after escaping from the sugarcane plantations at harvest time, more than one turned up armed with a machete. Who knew what harm they might do?

Siña Rosa did not agree with the men of the village. She was a widow who lived alone on a small plot planted with coffee, and she served as midwife and healer in the village. From time to time she would sit under a mango tree to chew tobacco and chat with the people passing down the road.

Next door to *siña* Rosa lived a young girl named Vitita. While she swept her patio and did other chores, Vitita liked to listen to *siña* Rosa's conversations with the men returning from Río Piedras with sacks of purchases slung over their shoulders, and the women carrying gourds full of water from the well. Vitita always listened quietly without saying a word. That way, she learned everything that was going on in the village.

While her brothers went fishing for freshwater shrimp in the stream, or looking for guavas in the orchard, or climbing up trees in the nearby woods, Vitita had to grate the cassava, sweep the patio, and mend her father's trousers. Her mother had died two years earlier. People said that her father would find himself a new wife, but no attractive girl of marriageable age could possibly think of marrying a widower with five children and very little land.

Vitita had been out of the village only twice, to go to religious festivals. She knew there were sugarcane plantations north of her village, and the road to the south led to Río Piedras. But beyond that town, the world was a mystery to her.

One morning Vitita's father got up early and went to town to sell plantains and herbs. He had been gone only half an hour when the hen sitting on her nest under the house fled in an uproar. Vitita thought a dog was trying to steal the eggs, and she ran to see what was happening. But it was no dog that she found crouching under the house, trying to rob the red hen's nest. It was a woman she had never seen before!

The two stared at each other silently. Vitita was frightened, but she could see the woman was trembling. She was a very dark-skinned black woman, about twenty years old, with high cheekbones and almond-shaped eyes. Her hair had not been combed, and her clothes were dirty and tattered. Though the heat of the day had not yet come, drops of sweat trickled down the woman's face.

"What are you doing under my house?" Vitita asked.

The woman peered out from the corner where she was hiding. An old kitchen knife tied to a rope around her waist glittered in the morning sun.

"Who are you?" Vitita asked.

The woman didn't answer. Instead, she ran away and disappeared into the woods.

Later in the afternoon, when *siña* Rosa was alone under the mango tree, Vitita told her what had happened that morning. When Vitita finished her story, *siña* Rosa spit out her chewing tobacco, wiped her mouth with her hand, and looked the girl straight in the eyes.

"Have you told your papa about this yet?"

"No, he's not back from town," Vitita said.

"Don't tell him a word, because men talk too much, and this could get to the wrong ears. I heard that an African slave escaped from a plantation in Puerto Nuevo yesterday. Did you notice if the woman had whip marks on her back? Did she speak our language?"

But Vitita didn't know.

Then *siña* Rosa told her what to do. Each night, after everyone had gone to sleep, Vitita should put a roasted plantain and half a gourd of sugarcane juice in the fork of the mango tree.

"What if Papa asks why I'm doing this?"

"Tell him I asked you to, so the wandering souls of the departed may have food on their journey," *siña* Rosa said.

Vitita did as *siña* Rosa suggested. The first two nights, no one touched the sugarcane juice or the plantain. But after the third night, the gourd was empty and the plantain was gone. From then on, the first thing Vitita did in the morning was to look in the fork of the mango tree. One night she left two ripe bananas, and the next, a baked sweet potato.

Vitita felt close to the woman she was helping. And so, one night, she placed the red comb her godmother had given her as a gift for Three Kings Day in the fork of the mango tree.

A week later Pedro Calderón came by to talk to Vitita's father.

"Good morning, my friend. They say there is a runaway slave in these parts. She's a dangerous one — slashed the foreman of a sugarcane plantation in Puerto Nuevo before she escaped."

"Well, I haven't seen any unfamiliar person around here," Vitita's papa said.

"Do you mind if I keep watch for her tonight from the top of your mango tree?" Calderón asked.

"You can watch as long as you want, my friend. Vitita will make you some hot ginger tea, so you don't become numb from the cold."

When Vitita heard that Pedro Calderón was trying to track down the runaway and that he was going to spend the night up in the mango tree, her heart fluttered with fear. She told her father she had to get a piece of ginger from *siña* Rosa to make the tea and ran to *siña* Rosa's house as fast as she could.

"Ay, *siña* Rosa! Pedro Calderón is here. He's going to tie up the woman and carry her away!"

"Don't you worry, my child," said *siña* Rosa as she handed her the ginger root. "Go back home and make your ginger tea. Just leave everything to me."

Siña Rosa went out and gathered dried tree branches from the woods. Late that evening she lit a bonfire near the mango tree. As soon as the fire was good and hot, she threw in fresh green branches. A cloud of white smoke heavier than a March wind rose and drifted over the mango tree. Pedro Calderón began to cough.

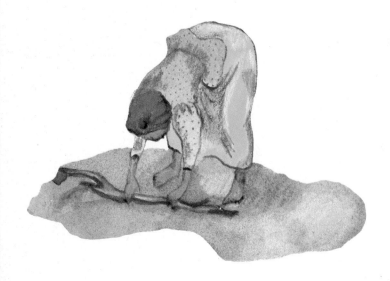

"*Siña* Rosa, *siña* Rosa, put out that blasted fire!" Calderón shouted.

"Who is it? Who is speaking to me?" asked *siña* Rosa as she added more green branches to the fire.

"It's me, Pedro Calderón," he said, coughing and choking.

"For goodness sake, why are you sleeping up in a mango tree?" said *siña* Rosa, throwing another piece of wood on the fire. "I thought a ghost was calling me!"

Pedro Calderón didn't know it, but there was a hornets' nest in the mango tree. Just then, the hornets, disturbed by the smoke and by Pedro Calderón's cries, swarmed all over him and began to sting. Coughing and screaming in pain, Pedro Calderón clambered down the mango tree.

"Ay, my friend, who'd have thought you liked keeping the owls company?" *siña* Rosa chided him. "Come over here so I can put some warm compresses on all those swollen bites."

The next day Pedro Calderón came to Vitita's house with two big dogs. "I know that runaway must be in these parts, and someone is feeding her," he said to Vitita's father. "Let me stay under your house with these two dogs. When they bark I'll let them loose so they can trap the runaway."

"That's fine with me, but at least have a cup of coffee first. Vitita, bring some coffee for my friend here."

"Yes, Papa. But we are out of brown sugar. Let me run over and ask *siña* Rosa for some," Vitita said.

She hurried to *siña* Rosa's to tell her about Pedro Calderón's two dogs. "What do we do now?" she asked.

"Evil cannot last forever, my child," *siña* Rosa reassured her. "I will find a way to solve this problem. Here's your sugar."

Vitita returned to her home while *siña* Rosa sat and thought. Just then a sad-looking young man passed by.

"What's the matter, Antón?" *siña* Rosa asked.

"I want to serenade my girl, but the guitar players charge two *reales* for a song."

"I'll lend you the two *reales* if you get me a dozen big-sized *bruquenas*, freshwater crabs, from the creek," *siña* Rosa promised.

In one hour Antón was back with a dozen big *bruquenas*. "Enjoy your *bruquenas* with rice, *siña* Rosa," he said.

"Oh, I will," said *siña* Rosa. She chuckled as she handed him the two *reales*.

Pedro Calderón hid under Vitita's house that evening, but he was unable to fall asleep. It was a dark, moonless night, and a blanket of clouds covered the stars. The dogs were restless. Strange noises were coming from the woods, and an owl hooted in the trees.

Pedro Calderón was not an easily frightened man, but he remembered a story he'd heard about a murder that had taken place nearby. At that very moment, Calderón spotted a lit candle moving by itself across the patio.

"Oh, no!" Calderón cried. "What if it's the soul of the dead man?"

The dogs growled.

Another candle followed right behind the first.

Calderón felt the touch of a hairy spider on his bare arm. He brushed it off with a startled cry. A cold shiver ran up his spine.

The dogs started to bark when the third candle appeared. Pedro Calderón didn't dare let them loose for fear the soul of the departed might haunt them. Then a fourth candle came into view, and a hoarse voice moaned: "Unnnder! Unnnder the house!"

Pedro Calderón let out a piercing scream. He jumped up and ran as fast as his legs could carry him, leaving the two dogs still tied to their posts.

The next morning Pedro Calderón came back to fetch his dogs. The animals had barked all night long, and no one at Vitita's home had slept a wink. Vitita's father suggested that Calderón hunt for the runaway slave somewhere else.

A few weeks later, *siña* Rosa announced to her neighbors that she'd heard from her sister in Cangrejos. She was sending her daughter Carmela to spend some time in the village—to get over the pain of a broken heart. "My niece is very shy and hardly talks," *siña* Rosa said, "but in time the girl will get over her heartache."

Two days later *siña* Rosa introduced her guest. She was very dark skinned, about twenty, with high cheekbones and almond-shaped eyes. She wore a freshly ironed white blouse, and her hair was neatly held back by a red comb and a pretty flower.

Vitita smiled every time she looked at the comb.

The news that Pedro Calderón had run away from the *bruquenas* spread quickly. No one ever dared mention it to his face. But a saying became common in the village: "Faster than Pedro Calderón running away from the *bruquenas*."

Carmela lived with *siña* Rosa until a young man from the village fell in love with her. They married and raised a happy family. And they loved to fill the neighborhood with the African rhythms of *bomba* music, especially on feast days.

Many years later, when Vitita herself was an old woman, she would tell her grandchildren stories about *siña* Rosa Bultrón. And of all the stories, their favorite was the story of the red comb.

The Red Comb takes place in Caimito, a rural district of Río Piedras, Puerto Rico, in the middle of the last century. The story is a fictional creation of Fernando Picó, but it is based on true facts and real people carefully documented in historical sources.

Among papers found in the General Archives of Puerto Rico for the years 1842–1849, there are two references to a Pedro Calderón, a mulatto from the Caimito district who obtains a reward of eight *pesos* for the capture of each fugitive slave he turns over to the authorities.

Esclavos, prófugos y cimarrones [*Slaves, escapees, and runaways*], a book of documents edited by Benjamín Nistal, includes files about fugitive slaves and about the hardships of their pursuit and capture. There's also a letter complaining about the lack of cooperation from the people in the Guaynabo area concerning the slave catchers.

The name of the Bultrón family appears in the first parish registries in Río Piedras. The Bultróns were among the oldest residents known by name.

The Red Comb was the winning entry in the children's literature contest organized by Ediciones Huracán of Puerto Rico in 1987. The contest was created as a means of encouraging authors to write historical fiction for young readers. The book was published for the first time in Spanish as a co-edition with Ediciones Ekaré of Venezuela, and was adapted into English in the United States by BridgeWater Books, an imprint of Troll Communications L.L.C.

ABOUT THE AUTHOR

Fernando Picó was born in Santurce, a central district of San Juan, the capital of Puerto Rico. Ordained as a priest of the Jesuit order, he is currently a history professor at the University of Puerto Rico in Río Piedras. He has published six historical books and numerous research articles.

Since 1980, Picó has lived in the rural district of Caimito in Río Piedras and has written a book on the history of his community. From residents of Caimito, Picó has learned a lot about local folklore and customs. He has also heard many ghost stories and stories of runaways.

ABOUT THE ILLUSTRATOR

María Antonia Ordóñez was born in Cuba and has lived in Puerto Rico since 1961. She studied fine arts at the University of San Juan, the Institute of Puerto Rican Culture, and several art academies. She has been awarded a number of honorary mentions and scholarships for her work, and her exhibits have been received with wide acclaim both in Puerto Rico and the mainland United States.